VICTORIA REX

THE INFINITY ENGINES

ANDREW HASTIE

Published by Here Be Dragons Ltd.

ISBN: 978-1-0683098-4-7

March 25 2.0

Other books in the Infinity Engines universe.

The Infinity Engines

1. Anachronist
2. Maelstrom
3. Eschaton
4. Aeons
5. Tesseract
6. Contagion
7. Tempest

Infinity Engines Origins

Chimæra

Changeling

Infinity Engines Missions

1776

1888

Victoria Rex

1

Kensington Palace 1834

Princess Alexandrina Victoria sat at her desk, studying the textbook while her tutor espoused the many virtues of the fossils he discovered on his last expedition.

It was terribly boring and the man smelled of mouldy cheese. She stared out of the window which looked out towards Kensington Gardens, wishing the lesson would end so that she could ride out in the autumn sun.

His name was Gideon Mantell and he'd apparently found the remains of a large reptile called *Hylaeosaurus* in Sussex the previous year.

Victoria had hoped to meet Mary Anning, the famous fossil huntress of Lyme Regis. Mary had discovered the *Ichthyosaur* when she was twelve years old and went on to be the first to find a complete *Plesiosaurus*. But the Duchess and Sir John forbade it, stating that it was not an appropriate profession for a woman – especially one that profited by selling her finds, which also seemed to be the opinion of the wider scientific community including the Royal Geological Society.

Ichthyosaur meant 'Fish Lizard' in Latin, which was one of the many languages she was learning in preparation for her role as the future Queen. Her uncle, King George IV, had died four years ago, making her the "Heir Presumptive", and elevating her overbearing mother into the role of regent, should his brother, William IV, not last until her eighteenth birthday.

Sir John Conroy, her mother's private secretary and possibly Victoria's least favourite person, was most insistent that she be educated in all the sciences, including palaeontology.

Victoria welcomed the news of a visiting tutor. Conroy's "Kensington System" meant she met very few new people. It was a strict set of rules that took away any chance of an adventure. She slept in the same room as her mother, and had to be accompanied down every step of the staircase.

Unfortunately, Mantell was something of a disappointment when he arrived. A balding middle-aged man with hollow eyes, nothing like the handsome explorer that she had read of in her books.

The bones of his discovery were laid out on the table before her. They were like ugly lumps of ivory, larger than anything she had ever seen. It took two of her strongest gardeners to carry them up to her study – both were less than happy about it, but then they complained about most things.

'As you can see from this fragment of tibia,' Mantell droned on, producing a pair of brass callipers, 'I estimate that the creature would have been at least twenty-five feet in length and over eight feet tall.'

'Fascinating,' said Victoria, stifling a yawn. 'And how long ago did it walk upon the Earth?'

The man looked slightly taken aback by the question. 'Well, that is open to a great deal of interpretation, your Royal

Highness. Some believe that the strata of rock it was found in could be millions of years old, while others say hundreds of millions.'

'I have studied Smith's geological surveys.' She nodded towards a bookcase filled with leather bound volumes. 'I found it most interesting, that the Earth should be so much older than the bible would have us believe.'

Mantell's cheeks were flushing as he struggled for an appropriate answer. Victoria knew he would have been instructed to avoid certain subjects, including religion.

'I, I, — '

'Alexandrina, do not tease the poor man!' rebuked her governess, Louise Lehzen, a Hanoverian baroness, who was sitting quietly by the window reading her bible.

'Never mind,' Victoria said, closing her textbook. 'Dash! Where have you been? Would you like one of these bones for your supper?'

Her King Charles Spaniel was nuzzling into her leg. He was a gift from Conroy in January, and was fast becoming her constant companion.

Mantell looked horrified. 'These are some of the oldest remains ever found in England! I am writing a lithograph on it for the Geological Society.'

Victoria laughed, picking up her dog. 'And it will be a most riveting read I'm sure.'

There was a knock at the door.

'Enter,' declared Victoria, glad of the interruption.

'Your Royal Highness,' said her maid, curtsying to Victoria as she entered. 'Mr Mantell and the Baroness are requested in the Red Saloon.'

The tutor looked relieved. Her governess tutted and put down her book.

'And we were having so much fun,' the princess replied with a sarcastic tone. Lehzen glared at her.

'May I be excused?' he asked, bowing his head.

'Of course,' Victoria replied, putting Dash on the floor. 'Dash and I have much to discuss.'

The man escorted the Baroness from the room, leaving his Gladstone bag behind.

'Now, what do you think he keeps in there?' Victoria whispered to her dog, peering inside the case. 'More bones?'

2

1835, Capitol Hill, Washington DC.

Rufius Westinghouse wandered amongst the crowd, blending into the background as any good watchman should.

It began to rain, something it always seemed to do whenever he attended a funeral. Umbrellas sprouted like black dahlias in front of him, obscuring his view of the frock-coated men who were following President Jackson into the Capitol building.

The memorial service was to mark the passing of Warren R. Davis, the representative of South Carolina.

Somewhere amongst the milling crowd was Richard Lawrence, an English-born house painter from Virginia, who was suffering from mental illness, potentially caused by exposure to toxic chemicals in the paint.

At this moment, he believed he was Richard III of England and that the US Government owed him a great deal of money.

Whatever the cause, the man was carrying two loaded pistols and was intending to shoot Jackson in the back.

Rufius moved amongst the spectators, most of whom

were sheltering under the porticos of the grand building. They had come in their hundreds to pay their respects, or catch a glimpse of the seventh President of the United States.

Taking out an old, leather-bound journal, his almanac, Rufius turned to a particular page. Fate lines wove across the paper like threads of a tapestry, creating an animated display of potential outcomes. There were fewer than 20 minutes until the convergence and he could see the Copernicans were still tinkering, temporal glyphs and annotations appearing and disappearing just as quickly.

'Damn clackers,' he muttered under his breath, closing the book and putting it away.

This was the second time Rufius had watched Jackson enter the building. On the first visit, the President had died. Lawrence shot him at point blank range as he left the service.

As a Praetorian of the Watch, his job was to ensure that certain historical figures remained in power long enough to achieve whatever destiny or fate had in store for them. Not that his employers, the Guild of Copernicans, would ever use such terms. They preferred phrases like 'conditional probability' and 'covariance', making decisions about historical alterations based on percentages and statistical analysis.

Every action he took was carefully calculated by a department of actuaries, mathematically modelled a hundred different ways from Sunday.

And it drove him mad.

His current mission was to ensure that President Jackson would not die today.

According to the Copericans' calculations, that shouldn't happen until 1845, at the age of 78, when he would succumb to tuberculosis and heart failure, surrounded by his friends and family.

• • •

Rufius checked his tachyon, which hung on his waistcoat like a pocket watch. It was an essential piece of temporal equipment with a series of concentric dials that displayed time in ten different centuries, as well as a myriad of other uses that any respectable time traveller would need.

Two minutes and counting.

There was movement in the crowd, the large doors of the Capitol opened and Jackson's entourage appeared from the interior.

Feeling the timelines converging, Rufius moved closer. He scanned the crowds until his eye caught sight of Richard Lawrence stepping out from behind a column in the east portico.

'Here we go,' he muttered to himself watching the man pull a pistol and level it at the President.

The gun misfired.

'First fail,' noted Rufius, gritting his teeth. 'Walk away now.'

Someone in the crowd screamed, and time slowed.

Lawrence reached for a second pistol.

Jackson raised his cane as his security detail launched themselves at the assassin.

The second gun failed to fire too.

'What did I tell you,' muttered Rufius moving quickly through the crowd which was running in all directions. 'Should have gone with the dagger.'

The President struck Lawrence over the head and the man fell to the ground. Before Rufius could reach him, Davey Crockett appeared and pinned the man down as Jackson continued to rain blows on the prone figure.

Slightly taken aback, Rufius slowed and took out his almanac, checking the now stable timeline. Crockett wasn't involved in the first version of this event, but he played his part and that was all that mattered.

'That'll do,' he said with a satisfied sigh. 'Nothing like a bad batch of gunpowder to ruin a perfectly good weapon.'

It was a subtle change, but a necessary one. Having located the gunsmith where Lawrence would buy the pistols, it was a simple task to adjust the levels of saltpetre.

The man would spend the rest of his days in an asylum.

The notebook vibrated and a message appeared in copperplate in the corner of the page.

'Princess Alexandrina Victoria is missing, proceed to 1834 immediately.'

3

Cretaceous, 136 million years BC

Victoria awoke to the sound of screeching birds.

She found herself laying in a bed of ferns, in what appeared to be a jungle, although the nearest the princess had ever come to experiencing one were the gardens at Kew.

This place felt rather different; the air was very humid and stuffy, like a warm summer's day in the Orangery.

Getting to her feet, she surveyed her surroundings. A high canopy of trees shaded her from the sun, their trunks were thick, twice the size of the oldest oaks in Windsor and ten times as tall.

'I don't believe we're in England,' she said, looking around for her dog. 'Dash? Come here boy!'

The dog was nowhere to be seen.

The last thing she could remember was looking inside the tutor's case, there had been something quite interesting amongst his accoutrements, a brass watch with numerous concentric dials.

Something had happened when she pressed the button on the side.

The world around her had dissolved.

Victoria's head began to spin at the thought of it. Realising she was experiencing 'a touch of the vapours', she sat on a nearby log and breathed deeply until the sensation receded.

Looking down at her hands, she noticed there were fractal patterns on her palm where she had held the watch. It was red and angry, like the welt from a nettle rash. Pulling up the sleeve of her dress, the design extended along her forearm, reminding her of the tattooed natives of Java.

'Well, that won't do at all,' she told herself, pulling down the cuff to cover it up and looking around the clearing.

'Now, where exactly are we?'

After an hour of struggling through the dense undergrowth, Victoria decided the length of her dress was entirely impractical and removed it, which was not a simple task without her maids. Fastened at the back, the laces proved difficult to reach and took nearly half an hour of manipulation and ingenious use of sticks to unravel.

Freed from the protection of the many layers of silk she realised very quickly there were hundreds of biting insects that took quite a fancy to her naked skin. She tore the bottom half of her dress away and wore the top backwards lacing it up at the front like a shirt. Her pantyhose and stockings protected her legs and the stout ankle boots were more than adequate for the uneven ground.

Her mother would not have approved of her attire, but at this very moment, Victoria was quite enjoying the freedom.

Kensington Palace had become a prison since her uncle died. Wherever this was, it was a blessed relief from the domineering restrictions of being the Queen-in-waiting.

• • •

There were no obvious paths, nor any signs of civilisation at all.

Victoria started walking downhill, hoping to find a stream; without water she knew she would not last long.

It was hard going; the undergrowth was dense and seemed unwilling to give way. Without a blade, she was forced to trample it down with her boots in a most unladylike way.

The heat was oppressive and seemed to be increasing as the day went on. Her legs were tiring and she realised there had been little in the way of physical exercise in her daily routine, beyond a ride around the gardens after lunch.

Finally she found a trail, where something large and heavy had crushed everything in its path creating a convenient highway down into the valley below.

4

Kensington Palace, 1834

Rufius waited patiently at the gilded gates of the palace, watching the Royal Guard taking a turn around the manicured gardens. It was an elegant, Jacobean mansion overlooking Kensington Gardens and Hyde Park. Back in the 1730s, under the reign of King George II and Queen Charlotte, it was better known as the "Party Palace", because they would hold magnificent balls that would go on until dawn.

He had attended a few of them, which were rather marvellous debauched affairs frequented by the rich and famous of the eighteenth century – a very different use to that of Princess Victoria's time. It was a period that the Queen would later come to describe as 'dark and miserable'.

Her father, the Duke of Kent, had died shortly after Victoria's birth and her mother relied heavily on his equerry, Sir John Conroy, to oversee the household affairs as a 'Comptroller'.

Rufius had met his type before. An ambitious man who

climbed the ranks of the Army until he joined the Royal Household. There were rumours that he was the Duchess's lover, although that was never proved. After the Duke died, Conroy took over the running of the estate and played a major part in the strict "Kensington System" rules which Victoria came to abhor. It was clear that he was hoping to serve as regent to the young queen, should her uncle die before her eighteenth birthday.

The man cut a striking figure in his morning suit, eyeing Rufius with suspicion while the princess's governess, Baroness Lehzen, sat on a velvet chaise and composed herself. They were in the Privy Chamber of the King's State Apartments, a state room that had hosted many visiting dignitaries. Rufius knew it was an honour to be allowed so far into the State Apartments.

The newly created role of plain clothes detective was still treated with disdain amongst many of the aristocracy – as it was amongst the Metropolitan Police in general.

Playing the role of an inspector was just one of the many persona Rufius had mastered. Authority figures were more readily accepted, drawing less suspicion and making it easier to ask unexpected questions.

'Tell the officer what you told me,' Conroy said, putting his hand on the woman's shoulder.

Louise Lehzen was an austere-looking woman with sharp features, reminding Rufius of a bird of prey. A Hanoverian Baroness by birth, she would remain Victoria's companion for many years to come.

She cleared her throat and sat a little straighter, clearly not comfortable with the physical contact. 'The lesson was supposed to end at three o'clock. I was to collect her highness and take her into the garden for riding at three-thirty, but when I arrived the dog was alone, and there was no sign of her.'

'We've searched the house and the gardens,' added Conroy. 'She is not on the grounds.'

Rufius took out his almanac and pretended to write some notes. 'I see. And who was the last person to see her?'

'Gideon Mantell, a visiting naturalist.'

The name was vaguely familiar, Rufius wrote it down, adding two question marks to flag it as something for the Copernican monitoring department to start working on.

'And where is this Mantell now?'

'Also missing,' Conroy said, his lip curling slightly. The man was clearly having trouble controlling his anger, which was understandable, losing the next Queen of England was a treasonable offence.

'I would like to see the room,' asked Rufius, hoping that Conroy would leave him to it.

Victoria's rooms were located on the floor below the King's Apartments. Rufius was taken down the servants' stairs by the governess. The beautifully ornate King's staircase was clearly out-of-bounds to men of his standing.

Decorated in the regency style, the rooms were less grand than those of the State Apartments. Her playroom contained a large dolls house and an impressive collection of dolls. A spaniel lay asleep by the fire, patiently waiting for the return of his mistress.

The next room was the study, its walls lined with bookcases of leather-bound books. There were two desks and a large table in the centre of a Persian rug. Apart from the two tall windows it was clear there was only one other way out of the room.

'And she takes all her lessons here?' asked Rufius, walking around the table.

'Yes, Reverend Davys and I instruct her on moral and religious matters, but she is also taught history, geography, arithmetic, and languages. Sir John invites other tutors for specialist subjects such as the natural sciences.'

Rufius took out his almanac once more. The Copernican's reply to his query about Mantell was written in a fluid copperplate.

Mantell, Gideon Algernon. 1790-1852. MRCS FRS. Obstetrician, geologist and palaeontologist. [ANTIQUARIAN]

'Mantell was a palaeontologist,' he said, ignoring the fact that he was also a member of the Antiquarian Guid and one of their Order.

The governess gave a slight shrug. 'He was a man of science, a doctor I think. He brought a recent find to show Alexandrina – the fossilised bones of a large reptile.'

Rufius reminded himself that Victoria was not her first name, she chose to use her middle name when she became queen because it sounded more English.

'A dinosaur?'

She looked confused. 'I've no idea. Sir John thought it would be an interesting distraction.'

'Indeed. Where is it now?'

'The porters took it away when the room was cleaned.'

'You cleaned the room?' exclaimed Rufius, realising the concept of forensics had yet to become a part of standard police investigations.

The woman nodded, lifting her chin as if he had slighted her pride. 'It is customary to clean after every lesson.'

'I will need to see them,' he added calmly. 'Is there anyone else who attended the lesson? Other children?'

The governess shook her head. 'No, no other children. It is not allowed.'

'And this Mantell, you say he was called away?'

'Yes, there was a matter of payment, Sir John wished to discuss terms of employment, before they left for the theatre.'

'So she was alone?'

She looked down at her feet. 'I was absent too. It is not allowed.'

5

Cretaceous

The river was wide and shallow, the water ran clear and tasted sweet. Her Gillie had taught her to drink from the fast-flowing eddies on a recent visit to Balmoral.

Long silver fish swam lazily in the pools surrounding the large rocks and her stomach groaned at the idea of catching one, but they were too quick.

Victoria climbed onto a half-submerged boulder and removed her wet stockings, laying them to dry on the warm stone. Taking out the strange fruit she found earlier, she tapped the pod against the rock. The shell broke on the third try, unleashing a terrible odour of rotten meat.

She threw the fruit into the stream and hugged her knees.

'Don't cry,' she told herself. 'This is not the time.'

There was a crack of branches from the far side of the river, the large ferns shivered as if something were moving through it.

Victoria held her breath.

The armour-plated head of a creature broke through foliage. Standing over thirty feet high, the enormous reptile lumbered out into the river, bowing its long neck to drink from the water.

This was a saurian, thought the princess, remembering the lecture that Mandell had given her. It was a fascinating beast, the body covered in a hard, scaly skin that looked as if it could repel any weapon. A row of thick spines grew out of its head and along its spine to a tail that was decimating trees and bushes with its casual swaying.

Dinosaur, Victoria decided to name it, her Latin education finally finding a use, *Terrible Lizard.*

The beast seemed to pay her little mind as it lapped at the water like a dog.

There was another sound above them, like the screech of an owl. Victoria shaded her eyes looking up into the sky. In the distance a flock of bird-like creatures was winging its way towards her.

As they approached she could see how much larger they were. With long beak-like snouts and leathery wings, they looked terrifying. The lumbering beast lifted its head from the water and decided it would be wiser to make for the cover of the trees, its thick, elephantine legs making short strides across the river towards Victoria.

Seeing her chance, she hastily grabbed her stockings, and as the beast passed by, leapt onto its back, finding a suitable saddle between two of the larger spines.

6

British Museum, 1834

Montagu House was in the early stages of being remodelled. The wings of the original building were being replaced by the colonnaded Greek architecture that would become synonymous with the British Museum of the future.

Rufius knew better than to enter via the public entrance, queueing was for linears, the name the Order gave to those who travelled through time in the usual fashion at one second per second.

He walked around to what used to be known as the "King's library", but had been recently renamed the "Enlightenment Gallery".

The oversight of museums fell under the auspices of the Antiquarian Guild, a group of curators charged with curating the artefacts of antiquity. Historical objects were one of the Order's most reliable ways to navigate back into the past, their timelines acting like a routefinder to distinct moments in time.

To a time traveller, museums were nothing more than telephone directories or transit stations, allowing them to jump to key events in history.

Libraries had similar capabilities, although books had less of a 'range' than ancient artefacts. They were under the jurisdiction of the Scriptorians, who were constantly in dispute about the best way to index them.

The Enlightenment Gallery was a long room, its walls lined with glass fronted wooden cabinets holding the eclectic collection of Sir Hans Sloane. Everything from mollusc shells and dried plants to rare Roman coins were on display.

A bust of the seventeenth century benefactor sat at the far end of the gallery, greeting the visitors as they entered. Rufius was less interested in the exhibits and more in its curator.

Barnabus Potts kept an office here, one of the more senior Antiquarians in the Order, there were rumours that he was being considered for Grandmaster.

'Westinghouse,' the old man greeted him as Rufius opened the small wooden door marked "PRIVATE - KEEP OUT".

The man was a little over five feet tall with bushy sideburns and a thick moustache.

'Barnabus, how the devil are you?' Rufius replied, taking his hand and shaking it vigorously.

The curator shrugged and waved around the small study which was packed to the ceiling with boxes. 'You know the old saying: time slips by, but history holds firm.'

'And yet there's always time for a drink,' suggested Rufius, placing a bottle of brandy on his desk.

'A Gautier?' exclaimed Barnabus, picking it up and squinting at the label. '1762 no less!'

'Indeed,' added Rufius, 'I have a favour to ask.'

The curator opened a drawer and brought out two glass

tumblers. 'Must be a serious one to require a Cognac of this quality.'

He poured two generous measures and handed one to Rufius. 'May our journeys bend, but never break the timeline,'

'Amen to that,' Rufius said, raising his glass.

They both sampled the brandy.

'So, what can I do for you? Last I heard you were working for the Romanovs.'

Rufius shook his head. 'Ah, now, that was not one of my finest moments. That would need at least another bottle, if not two. No, I'm here to ask you about Gideon Mantell. I believe he's one of yours?'

Barnabus took another sip and sat down behind his desk.

'Mantell, you say.' He turned to a brass rolodex and began to flick through it. 'Name sounds familiar. Has he done something wrong?'

'He's missing, as is the Princess Alexandrina Victoria.'

The curator coughed. 'The Heir Presumptive?'

'One and the same.'

After a few moments, Barnabus pulled out one of the cards from the carousel and pushed his half-moon glasses up his nose.

'Here we go. Mantell, Gideon Algernon. Yes, he's been with us since 1822 when he found the first fossilised remains of an Iguanodon. Teeth, if memory serves.'

'Do you happen to have his current location?'

Barnabus frowned at the text. 'Well that's a little odd,' he added, handing the card over to Rufius. 'I've never seen anyone travel back that far. It must be a mistake. It's usually very reliable.'

Rufius studied the chronographic map that sat in a square beside the handwritten biography. The temporal glyphs were indicating a date in the early Cretaceous period.

'One hundred and thirty-six million years ago,' he said,

noting the coordinates in his almanac. 'Not much that can take someone back that far.'

'Do you think he's taken the princess with him?'

Rufius scratched his beard. 'I've no idea, but somehow I've got to find a way to check.'

The curator poured them both another Cognac and raised his glass. 'Good luck my friend.'

7

Cretaceous

The lumbering beast, which Victoria named 'Ivanhoe' after one of her favourite books, continued at a pace for over an hour before slowing to a speed that would allow her to dismount.

She had ridden horses since she was five years old. The armoured skin of Ivanhoe was no more uncomfortable than a saddle although riding astride was a very different experience to the usual side-saddle.

They had travelled quite a distance, reaching a wide grassy plain which appeared to stretch for miles towards a range of distant mountains.

At first, Victoria wondered if she had somehow been magically transported to the Dark Continent. The stories of Africa were filled with hot, humid jungles and terrifying creatures, but this leviathan was clearly not part of her Empire, leading her to the only other logical conclusion: that she must have fallen through time.

'We must find shelter and set a fire,' she said to the beast who was busily grazing on a large shrub. 'Who knows what creatures will appear after dark.'

Ivanhoe seemed blithely unaware of her existence, which suited Victoria. His size and armour were impressive, but it appeared he was as docile as a cow.

The mountains would take too long to reach, even if she could persuade the creature to walk in the right direction.

Behind them, the dense forest looked imposing. 'Not a place to revisit without good reason,' she told herself.

The light was fading quickly, and storm clouds were gathering to the East.

As dusk fell, she caught a flicker of firelight in the distance.

'Fire is surely a sign of civilisation,' she told herself setting off towards it.

8

Map Room, Copernicus Hall. 1868

Professor Eddington stood amongst a swirling nexus of timelines, his face a mask of concentration while his hands moved through the ribbons of energy like an orchestral conductor.

'Increase the Seldon compensation by point five per cent,' he instructed his actuaries who stood behind consoles around the edge of the room.

Rufius watched silently beside Lord Dee, the founder of their Order and several of the grandmasters from the other guilds.

Eddington was the Stochastic Professor of the Copernicans' analytical department, the ones responsible for maintaining the Infinity Engine, a complex algorithmic model of the last twelve thousand years.

'We're losing temporal cohesion,' remarked one of his staff. 'Bifurcation will occur by twenty-twenty five.'

The professor grimaced, shaking his head. 'Highly improbable! Have you checked the Bernoulli variants? I believe you'll find they have shifted into the upper range.'

The young man blushed a little as he checked his figures. 'Apologies master, I have adjusted the data.'

Eddington nodded, isolating one time stream with the careful movement of his hand and expanding it to fill the space around him.

'My lord,' he began, turning towards the founder. 'You see before you the predicted course of the continuum should Princess Alexandrina Victoria fail to ascend to the throne.'

Lord Dee stepped forward, stroking his beard as he studied the branching lines of the holographic model. At key points along its length, small nodes of glowing light appeared like knots in a rope. Temporal glyphs floated around them, using the long dates of the Holocene calendar.

'Since her uncle, William IV had no legitimate surviving children, the next in line was the Duke of Cumberland. He was a much less popular choice who would have failed to balance the tensions between the monarchy, parliament and the expanding middle classes.'

He ran his finger along one particular line, which changed colour and branched out into multiple lines. 'Queen Victoria's children and grandchildren married into the great houses of Europe, forging dynastic lines that affected the entire Western world.'

'As well as encouraging a period of invention, industrialisation and scientific discovery,' added the founder.

'She must be found, and the continuum repaired,' added Eddington sternly, moving his hand further along the timeline. 'There are dire consequences for the future, should the alliances she forged not come to pass.'

They could all see the catastrophe that waited in the not-too-distant future.

'According to the Antiquarians she may be trapped in the Cretaceous,' added Rufius.

Eddington waved his hands and the holographic model

disappeared. 'Have you managed to determine how that occurred?'

Rufius shrugged. 'Either she's suddenly discovered latent powers that we weren't aware of, or her tutor, an Antiquarian by the name of Mantell had something to do with it.'

'Perhaps there was a breach?' suggested Derado, the Grandmaster of the Draconians.

'Nothing has been reported,' replied Eddington.

The founder turned towards Rufius. 'Do you think you can find her?'

He nodded. 'Aye my lord, assuming I can find a way back, it's over a hundred and thirty million years.'

His master's eyebrows raised slightly. 'The deep past. You should visit Grandmaster Janvier, he may have something that could help.'

9

Cretaceous

It transpired that what Victoria assumed was a campfire was actually a series of braziers strategically positioned in a ring around the perimeter of a collection of tents.

She stayed in the shadows as she circled the encampment. Her heart beat faster at the sound of voices. The snippets that she caught sounded remarkably like Russian.

Moving closer, she could see a cluster of large cages at the centre of the base, and soldiers with unusual-looking weapons standing guard over them.

The low moans of the beasts imprisoned within made Victoria catch her breath. Trapped like the trophies of big-game hunters, the cages held various types of dinosaur.

Including one that looked remarkably like Ivanhoe.

Before she had a chance to formulate a plan, a pair of strong hands gripped her arms and lifted her off the ground.

'Unhand me!' she insisted, wriggling to free herself and kicking her heels into the man's shins.

He laughed, his voice was deep and his breath smelled of

sour beer. 'Mishka,' he muttered under his breath as he threw her over his shoulder. 'This is not a place for little bears.'

10

Collège Mazarin, Paris. 1800

'There are very few things that could transport someone that far back into the past,' mused Antide Janvier, the Grandmaster of the Société des Antiquaires.

'Such as?' Rufius asked, surveying Janvier's office, which was located in the clock tower of the oldest University in Paris.

The old Antiquarian paused before answering, his long fingers casually stroking a brass orrery which sat in the centre of the room.

'A Wyrrm, perhaps?'

Rufius snorted. 'A Time Worm? Have you lost all of your senses man? Do you know what it would take to ride one of those into the deep past?'

The Grandmaster shrugged. 'You've never been one to turn down a challenge.'

'True, but that would be akin to suicide.'

The old Frenchman took a wad of tobacco from a silver tin and placed it into a long-stemmed pipe. 'Anyway, what could possibly require you to go back that far?'

Rufius stepped closer and lowered his voice. 'I need your word that what I'm about to tell you doesn't leave this room.'

Janvier lit his pipe and puffed away, creating clouds of smoke. 'But of course.'

'We may have lost our Queen.'

'Which one?'

'Victoria.'

The Grandmaster raised an eyebrow. 'Ah, yes that could be tricky. How exactly did you manage that?'

Rufius grimaced. 'The last person to see her was one of ours, a palaeontologist by the name of Gideon Mantell.'

A flicker of recognition passed across Janvier's face. 'The name sounds familiar. A fossil-hunter no?'

'Yes, not a very successful one, he was a visiting tutor to the princess before her ascendancy.'

'And you think he's taken her back to the Cretaceous?'

Rufius shrugged his shoulders. 'They're both missing and his almanac is showing it as his last known position.'

'In that case, It think we may be able to help you,' the Grandmaster said, walking over to one of the many cabinets that lined the room and taking out an unusual key from a chain around his neck.

He opened one of the doors, revealing a hidden room, or rather a laboratory.

Rufius smiled, this was the fabled research division of the Société des Antiquaires, possibly the most secret of departments within the Order. These were elite engineers, master craftsmen in the art of temporal mechanics.

He followed Janvier through the portal. Teams of white-coated artificers were poring over complex contraptions, some of which were tiny, requiring multiple lenses to study, while others towered over them, resembling V2 rockets.

'We've been working with Templeton's Quantum

tunnelling equations.' Janvier said, waving a hand nonchalantly towards a group of scientists. 'It's proving to be rather successful in our long-range tests.'

The sound of an explosion distracted the old man for a moment, a billowing orange ball freezing in mid-air above a nearby experiment.

A field of energy shimmered around the workbench holding back the force of the blast, effectively pausing the moment.

'Impressive,' said Rufius.

'Time suppression. A necessary safety measure when you're playing with the fabric of the universe,' the Grandmaster replied, as if it were an everyday occurrence.

A team in ornate hazmat suits appeared from nowhere and began to extract the individuals from inside the bubble of energy.

Janvier continued towards the far end of the laboratory, finally stopping in front of a sphere of brass rings.

'Here we are.'

'What is it?'

'A Time Machine, well the nearest we'll ever come to one. It's more like a time tunnel; they're still working on a name for it.'

The issue with travelling back into deep time was the lack of artefacts, or Vestiges, as the Order called them. Without a man-made object all that was left were artefacts made mostly from rock or bone. The chronology of organic material was notoriously chaotic and unreliable. Only the stupid or the insane tried to weave with natural artefacts.

'How far back have you managed to go?' Rufius asked, walking around the orb. It was large enough for a man to stand inside, but he resisted the urge to try.

'To the end of the Cretaceous. Close to the K-Pg boundary,

sixty-six million years or so. Alixia De Freis is interested in using it for her extinction research.'

'Is she now? That doesn't surprise me. When you say we, I'm assuming you've tested this with a human subject?'

Janvier shrugged. 'Not so much a human, no. More of an automaton. The data it collected proved that the environment was safe. You will be the first – a pioneer!'

Rufius scratched his beard, considering his options.

'What do you use for targeting?'

'The twin of Mantell's almanac should suffice.'

That made sense, thought Rufius, the Copernicans kept a sympathetic twin of every almanac in existence, it was how they were able to communicate across vast spans of time. The connection had something to do with quantum entanglement, but he'd never bothered to grasp the finer details.

'And the return trip?'

Janvier produced a tachyon from his pocket. 'It's been modified,' he said, handing it to Rufius, 'we've added a homing signal that can re-establish the connection with this base unit'

Rufius took the watch and examined it closely. It was finely made, with several additional features, and it felt heavier than his old timepiece.

'I'm going to need to change into something less modern,' he said, taking off his coat.

11

Camp Sakharov, Cretaceous.

When Victoria awoke, she found both her hands and feet were bound with rough rope. There was a throbbing ache on one side of her head where the man struck her after she bit him. There would be a bruise no doubt, but it was nothing compared to the concussion that she suffered falling from her horse the previous year.

It was strange to be treated so roughly. No one would dare lay their hands on her, let alone strike their future queen – it was tantamount to high treason. Although she often imagined that Sir John would give his eye teeth to do so.

The guards had locked her inside one of the smaller cages, it smelled of dead things and there was evidence of something's meal littered over the floor.

'Your Royal Highness,' hissed a voice in the dark. 'Are you hurt?'

Victoria recognised the weaselly tones of Mantell. Her tutor's face appeared out of the darkness. She shifted herself into a position next to the bars. 'Mr Mantell, what the devil is going on?'

He placed a finger on his lips, his eyes begging her to lower her voice.

'Please, they'll hear us.'

She pouted. 'I don't care. Who exactly are *they*?'

One of Mantell's eyes was swollen and there was a cut above his lip.

'Russians, Bolsheviks to be more precise.'

'I can't believe that Tsar Nicholas would ever have condoned such a treatment of these poor creatures.'

'These are not men of your time. They are revolutionaries, from the Soviet Union, it would be wise not to reveal your identity – they are anti-monarchists.'

Victoria was confused. 'If not of my time, then when?'

Mantell paused. 'I'm afraid I cannot say. I am bound by strict laws.'

'You dare to defy the heir to the throne? What law is greater than mine?'

'These are the laws of consequence, they involve your future. I cannot jeopardise events by giving you fore-knowledge.'

She took a moment to consider his answer. It appeared the man was being quite serious, although he was quite clearly mad. 'Are you implying that you are a time traveller?'

'I am your highness. Although I have never travelled so far into the past.'

'Exactly how far have we travelled?'

'By my reckoning it would be at least one hundred and thirty million years.'

Victoria couldn't imagine such a vast number. The Reverend Davys always insisted the Earth was only four thousand years old, according to the bible.

'Are you responsible for my present predicament?'

He shook his head. 'No ma'am that was not my doing.'

'And these Bolsheviks, are they time travellers too?'

'I'm not sure. They certainly shouldn't be here, but they

are not of my Order. It appears they are collecting specimens, so I am assuming they will be returning to their own time at some point.'

'Then we must try and escape before that occurs. Do you have a plan?'

'I do not.'

'Are there others like you?'

'There are.'

'Will they not notice your absence and send help?'

He sighed. 'It is unlikely.'

12

Collège Mazarin, Paris. 1800

Rufius braced himself as he stood inside the rotating rings of the quantum machine. There was a strange prickling sensation as the oscillating fields of energy washed over him. They made a noise like the sharpening of knives as they whirled around him and he was beginning to wonder if the Wyrrm might not have been a better option.

He prided himself on his range. Rufius had always been able to travel back further than most of his peers. There were very few who could say they had travelled to the end of the last ice age, over twelve thousand years ago.

Only the Nautonniers, the Draconian exploration force, could claim to have a longer historical reach. Missions like this were their speciality, but the founder had entrusted it to him - and he was not the kind of man to defy an order.

No one had ever attempted to travel this far back. Their natural abilities had limits, and constructing a machine capable of such a feat was the stuff of legend. Only Janvier's team had the genius—and the audacity—to make it a reality.

. . .

Rufius was wearing a mix of fur and jute, a homespun material that the Antiquarian costumier assured him would survive the long journey. Modern textiles had a tendency to disappear when travelling back through the past; there had been more than one embarrassing situation in his career when he misjudged the dress code.

The same went for weapons, there was little point in taking anything back with him, he would have to improvise when he got there.

'Try not to focus on the rings,' instructed Janvier, moving a series of levers on his console. 'You may feel a little discombobulated, but it will pass.'

Rufius did as he was told, watching the fabric of reality begin to unravel around him. It was like the fraying of a rope, the strands of time unfurling, winding around his body. The chronology of the continuum stretched back into the deep past, a long line of coloured threads that wove through history with no end.

He took a deep breath and let his mind follow the path, feeling the world around him slip away. The rings moving so quickly now they were nothing but a blur.

In the space between heartbeats, the world stabilised and Rufius was standing in the middle of a camp surrounded by dinosaurs in metal cages.

The quantum fields dissipated and the resulting disorientation hit him hard, like a train. He fell to his knees. Suddenly someone shouted something in Russian and there were men running around in what appeared to be army uniforms.

He blacked out before they had a chance to knock him out.

13

Camp Sakharov, Cretaceous.

'Wake up!' whispered a girl's voice, somewhere behind the darkness.

Rufius hadn't felt this rough since Caligula's last birthday party, which lasted the best part of a month.

'Can you hear me?' asked the girl.

He groaned and rolled over. 'Yes, I can.'

Raising himself onto one elbow, Rufius realised he was in a cage. There were two others staring at him through the bars, one of which looked remarkably like the young Queen, albeit covered in dirt.

'Your Royal Highness,' he said, running his hand through his thick red hair in an attempt to look more presentable. 'Are you alright?'

She nodded, her eyes widening. 'I am. Are you here to rescue us?'

'I am indeed. Although it appears we are both in the same predicament.' Rufius tested the bars, which were made of an unusual metal – their timeline was non-existent.

It was dark outside. On the other side of the compound

there were guards standing around a fire drinking and laughing, From what he could hear, they were speaking in Russian.

Rufius turned towards Mantell, who looked as if he had put up a good fight. 'Do you know what's going on?'

The palaeontologist nodded. 'I believe this is a scientific expedition. They appear to be part of Sakharov's team.'

Rufius looked confused. 'Andrei Sakharov? The quantum physicist at the Lebedev Institute?'

'He's managed to establish a wormhole here. From what I can ascertain they've been shipping specimens back to the late twentieth century.'

Victoria cleared her throat. 'Am I to understand that these poor beasts are being experimented on?'

'Most likely,' said Mantell.

'That's not my problem ma'am,' added Rufius, 'my first priority is to ensure your safe return to Kensington Palace.'

The princess frowned and folded her arms. 'I have no desire to exchange one prison for another.'

'I have my orders ma'am. I know it's not ideal, but it won't be for much longer.'

Her eyes widened. 'Really? Aren't you supposed to keep such things a secret?' She glanced towards her tutor. 'Mr Mantell informs me that there are strict rules.'

Rufius chuckled. 'I had a hand in writing most of them. Some are more just guidelines.'

'How do you propose to get us out of here?' asked Mantell. 'Are the Draconians coming?'

'No, at least, not as far as I know.'

Getting to his feet, Rufius went to the cage door and examined the lock. 'Your highness do you by any chance have a hairpin?'

Victoria nodded, removing one from her head and handing it to him through the bars. 'And who exactly are the Draconians?'

He took it and began to bend the metal. 'Soldiers of sorts,

explorers of the forgotten parts of history, brave souls, if not a little foolhardy.'

Rufius pressed himself against the bars of the cage, inserting the reshaped pin into the outer lock.

The door opened with a satisfying click and in less than a minute he had freed the others.

'It will be dawn soon,' Mantell said, looking up at the purpling sky.

Rufius took out his tachyon and tapped the dials. 'It would probably be wise to move to a safe distance before I try this.'

'We have to free them first,' insisted Victoria, pointing to the caged dinosaurs. 'I can't in all good conscience leave them behind.'

'I will come back and free them once you are safe,' he assured her.

She shook her head. 'We must do it now.'

Rufius shrugged and turned to Mantell. 'Any suggestions?'

The guards appeared to be sleeping by the fire. Rufius took his time, keeping to the shadows as he skirted around the outer edge of their camp. He counted at least twenty of them, each with some form of weapon, before making his way back over to the larger cages.

The beasts were all wearing a collar, which he guessed was some kind of pacifying device. Releasing one wouldn't be the hard part; the real challenge would be avoiding becoming the first course on their menu.

14

Camp Sakharov, Cretaceous.

They moved silently between the cages, careful not to wake the sleeping creatures. The enclosures formed a circle around a central area where a large sphere floated silently above the scorched ground. It held a distorted image of another world, one filled with machines.

'Wormhole?' wondered Rufius, walking over to it.

He could feel the energy fields pricking at his skin as he approached. They were nothing like the breaches he'd experienced before; they were holes punched into the fabric of the continuum by the nightmarish creatures of the Maelstrom.

Like a lens, the surface of the bubble showed a window onto the world beyond. He could see men in protective suits standing at consoles, adjusting dials and taking readings.

'Ivanhoe!' cried Victoria, running over to one of the cages.

'Quiet!' hissed Rufius, but it was too late, the captive dinosaurs rose as one, their deep, guttural roars would have woken the dead.

The sleeping guards jumped to their feet and sounded an alarm, more of them appeared from the tents.

Rufius chose the nearest cage and quickly picked the lock. The beast within ran at the door, which he used as a shield, only just managing to tear the collar from its neck as it passed.

'Tyrannosaurus Rex,' he murmured as it padded off towards the sound of the alarm bell. 'That should keep them busy.'

Victoria was standing by a smaller cage, talking quietly to a long, armour-plated creature.

'Ma'am, we have to go,' insisted Rufius, looking around for Mantell.

'We need to release them all,' she said, patting Ivanhoe's snout.

The tutor appeared from the shadows, carrying a small egg. 'They're dangerous beasts, ma'am, most of them are herbivores, but there is still a chance they may trample us.'

'I don't care!'

Rufius could hear the screams of the guards as they tried to fight off the T-Rex. It wouldn't take long for it to finish playing with its food.

'Fine,' he said, unlocking the door of Ivanhoe's cage. 'But leave the collars on. By the time my friend is finished his breakfast they'll be little use.'

Most of the dinosaurs wandered out of their cells and into the dawn, hardly noticing the humans that freed them.

Victoria walked Ivanhoe to the edge of the camp and patted its rump, like a horse being set free into a field.

'Now,' she said on her return. 'Are we going through the looking glass?' Pointing at the bubble of the wormhole.

Rufius was suddenly struck by the similarities to Alice in Wonderland, but that wouldn't be published for another forty years in her time. Perhaps she told something of her story to Liddell later in life.

'No, I have one of my own,' Rufius replied, taking his tachyon from inside his furs.

15

Chapter House 1868

Victoria's dress was being restored by the Antiquarian costume department, while she ate a hearty meal at the Chapter House, courtesy of the De Freis family.

Their host, Alixia, was very interested to hear their story. She was as a xenobiologyst with a fascination for the extinction of the dinosaur and Mantell's egg was a particular attraction. While dinner was served, negotiations were underway at the other end of the long table.

It took a while, and the best part of a bottle of Chateau Margaux, but Rufius finally remembered where he heard the man's name. He was a relic trader, someone who profited from the selling of ancient artefacts.

His speciality was fossils. It wasn't strictly legal, but generally overlooked by the Protectorate, since there was little advancement to be made from selling iguanodon teeth.

What was really bothering Rufius was how Victoria ended up in the Cretaceous in the first place.

There was clearly a Russian experiment which needed to be closed down, but how she had accidentally found herself a hundred and thirty-three million years in the past was a mystery.

'How was the trip?' asked Methuselah, Alixia's husband, refilling Rufius's wine glass. 'I think you may have set a new record.'

'Like I got dragged through a hedge backwards by a herd of wildebeest.'

Methuselah laughed. 'Well, Alixia can't wait to try it, she's already planning a trip back to the Pliocene.'

Rufius chuckled. 'You'll need to take some serious precautions. From the little I saw of it, everything will try and kill you.'

Her husband grinned, looking over to his wife. 'Oh, I think they're the ones that should be worried.'

Victoria was chatting to Lyra, Methuselah's daughter, it was the first time Rufius had heard her laughing. Strange to think that her mother kept her away from other children.

'Do you know how she ended up back there?' asked Methuselah.

'Not yet. She says she was looking through Mantell's stuff and passed out.'

'Have you had her tested?'

'You think she may be a latent?' said Rufius, taking out his almanac and opening it on a page displaying her timeline. 'I didn't see anything in her record, maybe I'm losing my touch.'

His host shrugged. 'There have been cases. It wouldn't be the first monarch with our abilities. Who knows, maybe she's a druid?'

Druid was the nickname they gave to those who could weave with the timelines of organic materials, the skill was rarer than hen's teeth, but there were a few.

Rufius closed the almanac. 'She's certainly resilient. Most

girls of her age wouldn't have lasted a day. But I doubt it. More likely is that Mantell's been up to something. The Russians have developed some kind of wormhole technology. It wouldn't surprise me if he's been buying fossils from them.'

'Shipping dinosaurs back to present,' Methuselah mused, carving a slice of meat from the roasted pig sitting in the middle of the table. 'I've always wanted to try some Carpathian Boar,'

Rufius choked on his wine. 'You know I never thought of that! You think the Russians are harvesting them?'

Methuselah shrugged. 'There's a lot of prime meat running around back there, who knows how much it would sell for on the black market.'

Kensington Palace, 1834.

Sir John Conroy was visibly relieved to see Victoria when she was returned unharmed. Her mother, the Duchess, was verging on hysterical.

Rufius could have brought her back to a point in time before they noticed she was missing, but he wanted to teach them a lesson.

Six hours had passed since he left the palace, just long enough for them to begin to reflect on their treatment of her.

The Order's redactors wiped the memory of her time in the Cretaceous, and Doctor Crooke had healed the cuts and bruises with one of his usual foul-smelling concoctions.

The official story was that Mantell had abducted the princess. That he was arrested at Euston station and was currently undergoing treatment at a sanatorium for the mentally unstable.

'He should be hung, drawn and quartered,' growled Conroy, gripping his cane with white knuckles.

Rufius made his excuses and left.

16

Red Bar, Pyatnitskaya Street

It took Rufius a while to track down the location of the lab, Soviet science institutes were notoriously secretive and well-guarded.

Mantell finally admitted that he was buying fossils from the Russians, the Antiquarians tested the bones that he claimed was *Hylaeosaurus* and confirmed that their sub-atomic structures were still in a state of temporal flux, consistent with quantum manipulation. The theory was that Victoria had been playing with Mantell's tachyon in close proximity to them and the tutor had tried to stop her, getting caught in the temporal aperture it created.

He would be spending the foreseeable future under close scrutiny by the Protectorate, a temporal form of house arrest.

It transpired the dealer that Mantell bought the fossils from was a sleazy character by the name of Yuri Gorgoroff. He worked at the Institute as a porter, but was making a tidy profit in stealing the bones from the labs and selling them on the dark market. Discerning collectors would pay handsomely for the remains of previously undiscovered species.

. . .

They met in a dingy bar on Pyatnitskaya Street.

Gorgoroff was clearly an avaricious man, his large round belly a sign of overindulgence. He had greasy, black hair that was obviously dyed, and there was an air about him, he was never able to look you directly in the eye.

'You want a T-Rex?' he said with a thick Russian accent. 'It's going to be expensive.' He rubbed his thumb and forefinger together. 'Many dollars.'

'I can afford it,' Rufius assured him. 'When?'

The man rubbed his chin. 'There's been some trouble with supply, may be a month, maybe longer.'

Rufius realised that their escape must have affected production. Whatever was going on inside the Institute, losing a team was going to have consequences. No one would want to volunteer knowing that the last crew were wiped out by the very thing they were supposed to be hunting down.

'You want something else,' the man asked, leaning forward. 'I got some beautiful Velociraptor teeth, or maybe Triceratops horn?' he added, raising his arm with a balled fist and smirked. 'Very rare, the Chinese go crazy for them.'

It wouldn't take much to go back and adjust the man's timeline, thought Rufius, a small adjustment in his father's past and the dealer would be nothing more than a twinkle in the old man's eye.

The watchman shook his head. 'I heard a rumour that you do tours, for special customers.'

The Russian laughed, sitting back in the couch and taking out a cigar, which looked liked a Regius Double Corona, a custom-made smoke that would have cost over ten thousand dollars in this time, more than ten years wages in communist Russia.

He lit the cigar. 'You heard? From who?'

'Mantell.'

Gogoroff nodded his head, blowing out a cloud of smoke. 'So you know Mantell. He's a good man. A good customer. Yes, I can get you inside, but it will cost.'

'Many dollars, I know.'

Lebedev Physical Institute, Troitsk, Moscow. 1964

A mile beneath the streets of Moscow, and over a thousand dollars in bribes, they reached a pair of blast doors that reminded Rufius of a nuclear bunker.

It took Gorgoroff several minutes to open the complex locking mechanism, as the gears ground into action the thick doors retreated to reveal a terrible zoo.

The chamber beyond was a vast hangar filled with large metal cages. The cries of the creatures resonated through Rufius's bones as the gigantic beasts paced around inside them. All were wearing the pacifying collar, but some had other devices embedded in their skulls.

'Welcome to Jurassic Park,' Gogoroff joked tapping the bars with his ringed fingers. 'Is a freakshow, no?'

'It is indeed,' sighed Rufius, watching a triceratops lumber towards them. 'What are you doing to them?'

The Russian shrugged nonchalantly. 'Comrade Sakharov created a gateway into another time, one filled with monsters. We look for ways to control them.' His eyes glinted. 'Maybe use them against our enemies.'

They're trying to weaponise dinosaurs. Rufius realised. *Who needs ballistic missiles when you've got a battalion of Tyrannosaurus Rex.*

'Where is Sakharov?'

Gorgoroff eyes dropped to the floor. 'KGB took him. He's probably in Siberia by now.'

Rufius had all the evidence he needed.

The case for changing the timeline was clear, the Copernicans would have no trouble sanctioning the adjustment. He would go back and stop Sakharov from developing the wormhole technology. A subtle modification to one of his early experiments or a series of failed prototypes would be enough to ruin any chance of success. It might also keep the scientist from being sent to one of the worst gulags on the planet.

As for the fat fossil dealer standing before him, Rufius was trying very hard not to throw him in one of the cages – it would be a fitting end for the bottom feeder.

Instead, he took a large wad of dollar bills from his pocket. 'As agreed,' he said, handing them over. Gogoroff smiled and began to count the notes, licking his thumb every so often.

When he was done he held out the same hand to shake on the deal.

'A pleasure doing business with you.'

Reluctantly, Rufius shook it. His fingers gripping hard, touching the man's rings. It took less than a second to find the right timeline amongst them. The ring that had once belonged to Gogoroff's father.

Another second and Rufius located the exact moment, disappearing into thin air, shortly followed a moment later by a confused-looking fossil dealer.

17

28th June, 1838. Westminster Abbey. London

According to the Copernicans' conservative calculations, there were four hundred thousand people lining the streets to watch Queen Victoria's procession.

Rufius would have put it higher. It brought London to a standstill.

Her gold state coach left Buckingham Palace and made its way past Hyde Park Corner and up Piccadilly towards Westminster Abbey.

He joined the entourage earlier that morning, joining the ranks of the Yeoman of the Guard – the Queen's close protection unit. Wearing the red and gold uniform and carrying the partisan, a ceremonial halberd, over his shoulder, Rufius marched proudly behind the carriage.

They progressed slowly along the crowded streets taking over an hour to reach the abbey.

The Yeomen Guard lined up on both sides of the steps to the Church, creating a protective barrier between the crowds and her majesty, who stepped gracefully down from the carriage. Dressed in a simple white satin gown, she looked so different from the girl he left in Kensington Palace a few days ago. Four years had passed in that time, but the woman before him still carried the same look of determination.

She stopped for a moment to wave to her subjects, catching his eye as she did so.

For a moment there was a glimmer of recognition, a question forming on her lips, and Rufius wondered if the redaction had not been quite as thorough as it should have been.

The moment passed, she smiled and nodded before being escorted into the Abbey by the Lord Chamberlain.

Rufius turned with the others and followed her inside.

It was the beginning of one of the longest reigns of any monarch, he reminded himself as the fanfare began. He knew what was to come, and although it was overshadowed by the loss of her beloved Albert, it would be one of the most memorable periods in British history.

And this was not to be the last time they would meet.

But that is another story entirely.

THE
INFINITY
ENGINES
ANACHRONIST
ANDREW HASTIE

PROLOGUE

This short story serves as a prelude to Anachronist, revealing some of the events, characters, and conflicts that set the stage for the first book in the series. It provides insight into the world and hints at the mysteries to come...

1

THE DAY OF FOUR PARTS

Rufius always thought of a day as having four parts.

Although the word "day" was a rather loose term for a man of the watch. There were pitifully few times in his long service for the Oblivion Order when he could remember experiencing one from sunrise to sunset.

The luxury of remaining in linear time for twenty-four hours was something to be savoured, even though it generally meant dealing with the more mundane tasks, like shaving, washing clothes and general housekeeping.

The first part, which he liked to refer to as 'Promising', covered an initial period from waking until his stomach insisted it was time to eat. This was a time of awakening both of mind and body, and usually involved checking to see which century he found himself in and whether anyone was trying to kill him.

Promising could go either of two ways, depending on the status of his almanac. Which Rufius tried to ignore until he'd eaten something. He learned from bitter experience that his capacity to deal with the catastrophic events that unravelled across its pages was greatly improved by a full stomach.

The almanac would remain closed until after the second cup of tea. Unless it was physically shaking, in which case there was something of an emergency.

It was an interesting book. Bound in age-worn leather, it contained his chronographs, the temporal maps of various missions within his domain. The complex branching lines of the twentieth century wove across the yellowing pages in real-time, as somewhere back in the sixteen hundreds, Copernican actuaries updated the outcomes of various historical events and their potential effect on the future.

Between the animating lines, messages scrawled themselves in fluid copperplate as if being written by an invisible hand.

The second phase of his day would either be 'Troublesome' or 'Agreeable', depending on these missives. Almost always there would be something that needed to be corrected. Some insignificant part of history that required a minor alteration to keep the continuum in check. These he classified as Troublesome, no matter how subtle the adjustment.

Today seemed to be one of the more agreeable days — a rare moment when he could spend a little time in his garden.

The house came with the job. A three-storey Victorian detached villa on one of the more desirable squares in South-West London. Inside, the upper floors resembled a museum, filled with artefacts collected from a thousand different missions, each carefully labelled and stored in his very own cabinet of curiosities. These were his most valued possessions, bookmarks that could transport him directly into the past by following their timelines.

The ground floor was not so well maintained, filled with books, manuscripts and papers from the last six hundred years, stuffed into every available nook and cranny. It looked like the home of a hoarder, as did the front garden, much to the chagrin of his neighbours, who took great pride in their neatly clipped hedges and were not impressed by the unsightly piles of junk that had accumulated beside them.

The back garden, however, was a sanctuary. There was nothing more agreeable to Rufius than spending part two of his day surrounded by the delights of his botanical haven.

He collected plants from all over the globe and through time, venturing as far back as the Pliocene for some of the larger ferns. With the help of Alixia De Freis, a friend who specialised in the curation of extinct species, Rufius had recreated an extravagant garden that rivalled the likes of Kew.

Alas, part two never lasted very long, since 'Troublesome' tended to have a terrible habit of rearing its ugly head. If something hadn't gone wrong by teatime, he would assume the link with his almanac was malfunctioning and call the Copernicans directly.

Sometimes, part three could last for weeks, but thanks to his tachyon, a watch-like device that kept track of his temporal location, he was able to return to the 'present' at roughly the same time as he left. Give or take a minute of two, for safety, since one never liked to meet oneself — closed time-loops were a nightmare to unravel.

The final part of his day involved drinking.

His work done, Rufius retired to his favourite period, his 'Forgetting' phase.

Sliding inside a bottle of whisky was the most efficient way he'd found to deal with the psychological effects of altering the past. Witnessing the near-collapse of reality tended to wear one down after a while. Many watchmen found it too much, retiring from active service after their first 'tour' of duty. Five years was the average for most. Rufius had lost count after twenty.

His head was filled with memories of things that never occurred: disasters that were averted, assassinations of dictators who would never rise to power, wars that never were. It was a dirty job, one that took no sides other than to ensure the best possible future for humanity. He did as instructed, an agent of the Oblivion Order, devoting their lives to protecting the best possible outcome for the future of the human race.

2

THE LIBRARY

Caitlin had lost a book.

Of course there were many lost books in the Great Library. It was the reason the Scriptorian Guild created the labyrinthine repository — to preserve knowledge that would otherwise have been lost to history. It boasted the entire collection of the Royal Library of Alexandria, Pliny's Naturalis Historia, as well as the lost works of Cicero, Aristotle and most recently, the Aztec codices burned by the Aztec emperor Itzcoatl.

Caitlin joined the Scriptorians the moment she reached the age of requirement. She loved books, not just the feel of the leather bindings or the musty smell of the old vellum, but the places they could take her.

The particular tome she misplaced was the only surviving edition of the Voynich Codex. She'd been tasked with researching its writing system by Master Howfall, the head of Linguistics. It was a fifteenth-century manuscript filled with fictitious plants, astrological symbols and fantastical illustrations that no one within the her guild had managed to decipher and the original author was proving mysteriously untraceable.

Caitlin was on a reading week. She was studying Ancient History at Oxford and was supposed to be working on her thesis on the Chinese General Sun Tzu, who was credited with writing the famous military strategy, 'The Art of War'. She'd spent the last few days travelling back into the Eastern Zhou period of ancient China, but when the opportunity to work with Linguistics popped up in her almanac, she dropped everything and applied.

She could imagine how Master Howfall would take the news of the missing book. Her chances of working in the elite cryptographic department would be over.

Walking between the stacks, she tried to retrace her steps. The vast towers of ancient books stretched up into the distant ceiling, where small figures moved on fine chains between them, like acrobats on the high wires of a circus.

Without realising, Caitlin found herself in Admissions, one of the more notoriously unorganised departments within the library, where all new arrivals were processed before being categorised, coded and placed into their relevant sections.

An old man was standing on a ladder leaning up against a pile of manuscripts at least three times his height.

'Miss Makepiece,' he said, sliding down the ladder like a man half his age. This was Grandmaster Chittenden, one of her grandfather's oldest friends and the longest-serving Head of Retrievals. 'I'm glad you dropped by. I was wondering if you would be interested in a little expedition we're planning into Villa dei Papiri?'

His long white eyebrows formed an arch over his nose, and one hand stroked the snowy beard that covered the rest of his face.

Caitlin knew of the Villa; it was infamous amongst the Scriptorians for the numerous failed attempts to retrieve the scrolls that were stored within it. Based in the small town of Herculaneum, the Villa had been buried during the eruption of Vesuvius in AD 79, which had wiped out Pompeii and thwarted all efforts to reach the eight hundred scrolls that were ninety feet deep below the ash.

The rules of retrieval were very specific: documents could only be removed at the point of obliteration; no linear should ever be aware they had been recovered before the disaster; anything that led to the revealing of the Orders existence was strictly forbidden.

Trying to rescue the scrolls while an erupting volcano rained fire down on the roof was not Caitlin's idea of fieldwork.

'Thank you, Grandmaster,' she said with a deferential bow of her head, 'but I'm afraid I will have to decline. I've been asked to join an exploratory mission into the lost library of the Tsars.' It was a lie of course, but to admit she was working with Linguistics would only lead to more questions, especially about a book she couldn't admit to losing.

His eyes glazed over. 'Ah yes, an equally important enterprise. Your mother and father would be so proud.'

She felt her cheeks warming at the mention of her parents. They'd been missing in action since she was ten, and although eight years had passed, she still hated it when people referred to them as if they were dead.

Quickly bidding him good day, she hurried away.

Taking a detour through Cartography, she stopped below the giant Armillary sphere that hung in the centre of the department, slowly rotating as it followed the rotation of the solar system in real time.

'Hey,' she whispered to a blonde boy who was watching the brass spheres twist slowly overhead.

'Hi Cat,' he said, without turning around. 'Did you know Saturn has a hexagonal shaped storm around its North Pole?' Her step-brother, Sim, had always been fascinated by the planets. From the age of eight, he could calculate the orbits of every astral body in the heavens with a slide rule and a sheet of paper. Which was probably why the Copernican Guild had inducted him into their actuary programme

'And its rings stretch one and twenty-thousand kilometres from the planet,' she replied. Their intellectual duelling was of many reasons why she loved him dearly. 'Were you looking for me?' she asked, catching sight of a book under his arm.

Sim snapped out of his reverie and turned, holding the Voynich Codex out towards her. 'Yes, sorry, I was just returning this.'

Frowning, she snatched it from him, inspecting the spine and covers for damage. 'I've been looking everywhere for this,' she exclaimed loudly, receiving a collective glare from the other readers in the department.

'Sorry,' said Sim, 'I needed to visit the court of Rudolf II around 1600, and the manuscript seemed like the quickest way to get there.'

'You realise it's not supposed to leave the library?'

He shrugged. 'Technically, it didn't. I just used its chronology.'

Books were like maps to the members of their Order; ancient ones could be used to move back through hundreds of years in a heartbeat. Using their timelines was far safer than wandering the uncharted timelines; that was the job of the Draconian Guild, and more specifically, the Nautonniers, the Guild navigators to which both her mother and father belonged.

She sneered. 'I signed this out. You realise what would have happened if they found out I'd lost it?'

'You'd lose your library card?' he joked. Copernicans took a dim view of the other guilds. They saw themselves as far superior to the others.

'I'd lose my job,' she hissed through gritted teeth.

His smile faded. 'Sorry, Cat, I should have asked. It was stupid of me.'

Caitlin couldn't stay angry at Sim for long. He was a kind-hearted boy who would do anything to help her. He'd been her best friend since she'd come to live with his family.

'So why have they got you going back to Prague?' she asked.

Sim shrugged. 'He didn't want to bother the Watch. Something's up with the Second World War. I haven't seen Eddington this excited since the fall of Rome.'

3

PREDICTIONS

Professor Eddington made a tiny adjustment to one of the controls and an entirely new set of lines branched out from the nexus floating in space before him.

Sim loved to watch his mentor work the algorithm. The professor's hands plucking at the threads of the continuum like a weaver, manipulating the timelines, teasing apart the continuously flowing ribbon of light.

The Copernicans were masters of prediction, using highly complex mathematical models to calculate the best possible future. It was a never-ending task, requiring the power of a computational engine the size of a cathedral, the building in which they now stood.

Eddington's hand suddenly froze over a single point in the network of lines, his fingers twitching to expand the event, magnifying it until the finer details were revealed.

'Master Simian, please apply the Heisenberg coefficient.'

Sim did as he was asked, watching the additional formulae strip away the less relevant factors until there were fewer critical timelines to focus on.

'Now the Malvarnian interpretation,' instructed the

professor, pushing his spectacles back onto the bridge of his nose.

Again the model changed, becoming a single thread.

Eddington's face was a study in concentration, his eyes nothing more than narrow slits behind his glasses.

Sim recognised the temporal sigils around the event. It was part of the first year syllabus in his actuarial studies — the Second World War.

'As I suspected, it appears we have a bifurcation, as predicted by Grandmaster Watzenrode.'

The Watzenrode hypothesis was a hotly debated subject amongst the senior Copernicans, which argued that there were two equally justifiable endpoints to the Second World War and, more specifically, to when Hitler was removed from power.

The first was his assassination during a meeting of his executive at Wolf's Lair in Eastern Prussia in July 1944, and the other was the fall of Berlin in April 1945.

The current timeline was running with the first scenario. Still, Sim could see from the predictive model that something was causing a change in the pattern.

'There seems to be a singular causation,' Eddington whispered, slowly moving his fingers through the lines of light, teasing apart the luminous strands. 'One particular change agent. Curious chronological pattern. Can you run a trace on this lifeline?' he asked, separating one pulsing thread from the others.

Sim nodded, moving his hands across the brass controls of his console, adjusting the dials and watching the glyphs of the temporal coordinates fall into place. 'Joshua Jones. Point of origin, 2000. London.'

Eddington looked confused. 'A member of the Order?'

Sim shook his head. 'Negative professor.' He knew from his mentor's expression what the next question would be.

'Who do we have on watch during the twenty-first century?'

Sim was already opening his almanac. He ran down the list of watchmen until he reached the twenty-first.

'Westinghouse.'

Eddington sneered, unable to hide his disappointment. 'Send the details to him, but I'm going to call for an emergency session of the High Council.'

Sim wrote Westinghouse's name at the top of a blank page, adding the glyphs for the timeline and watching the branching lines spreading across the paper. Somewhere deep below in the bowels of the Copernican headquarters, an entire department of actuaries would be busy transcribing the details onto a temporally linked copy of Westinghouse's almanac.

4

CHAPTER HOUSE

The Chapter House was unusually quiet for a Tuesday evening.

Standing at the bottom of the grand staircase, Rufius swayed drunkenly from one foot to the other staring up into the into hundreds of storeys. It was truly a marvel to behold, far more than the mid-terrace Georgian house that it appeared to be from the outside.

Methuselah De Freis, Alixia's husband, was a temporal architect, one with the skills to connect the existing rooms and floors to great houses of history, creating a staging-post-cum-hotel that could accommodate a thousand travellers with ease.

Methuselah also laid on one of the best meals in the continuum: Carpathian Boar roasted over a log fire in a Viking long hall which doubled up as their dining room. The De Freis household also boasted an extensive wine cellar. One advantage of being able to travel through time was a near infinite supply from the best cellars history could offer.

'Uncle Rufius?' said Caitlin, stepping through a small arched door in the wood-panelled hallway. 'Are you okay?'

'Ah, my dear Caitlin,' he said, performing a drunken bow. 'Where's everybody else?'

'Haven't you heard?'

Caitlin could tell from his blank expression that he had not. 'Sim said there's some kind of major disruption in 1944. Where's your almanac? You should've received a message.'

Rufius shrugged, searching his pockets and producing a bottle of brandy. 'Must've left it in my other coat,' he added before pulling the stopper out with his teeth. 'What's happened?'

'I think you've had quite enough of that,' she said, gently taking the bottle from his hand. 'Let's get you some coffee before we go to the High Council. Eddington has called an emergency meeting.'

She took his hand and led him down the hall towards the dining room.

'Is there any boar left?' he asked, following like a dutiful child.

Rufius became her guardian when her parents went missing eight years ago. He was a good man, a perfect mix of bodyguard, mentor and clown. Even when she struggled with hormone-driven teenage angst, he was her rock, never blinking an eye as the rage and hate poured out of her.

But he was troubled too. Caitlin knew many within the Order thought he was past his prime, that he was fighting too many demons.

The drinking was something he'd struggled with for a long time. His "forgetting potion" she used to call it when she was younger. It wasn't until later that she understood why Rufius insisted she stay with the De Freis at the Chapter House.

His life wasn't suited to raising a child. The job of a

watchman was usually taken by men and women with nothing left to lose. Witnessing the change of history came with psychological damage, and no matter how much he joked about it, she knew he was carrying a lot of scars.

Especially since the death of his wife and child.

5

COUNCIL

The Grandmasters of the various guilds sat in high-backed thrones on a dais that curved around half of the circular star chamber. Wearing sombre expressions, they listened while Professor Eddington explained the gravity of the situation in 1944.

Around the ranked rows of the auditorium, members of the Order appeared in their seats, the benches quickly filling with an assortment of strangely dressed individuals from various parts of the last thousand years.

Rufius watched Eddington pacing around the chequered floor in his dark robes, his hands behind his back like a priest rehearsing a sermon.

His head was slowly clearing, thanks to Caitlin's insistence on three cups of strong coffee and one of Doctor Crooke's foul-tasting tonics. She'd also found his almanac, which did indeed have an urgent message, and she duly responded in a worryingly convincing imitation of his handwriting.

. . .

The Grandmasters were accustomed to long monologues from the Head of the Copernican Statistical Analysis Division. However, it was clear that some were beginning to lose patience, including the Leader of the Council and the founder of their Order, Lord Dee.

'What is your considered opinion as to the best course of action?' the founder asked, getting to his feet.

Eddington was clearly caught off-guard by the interruption, his mouth flapping like a fish as he considered his answer. Rufius tried his best not to laugh, but only Caitlin's nails in his leg stopped him.

'Surely the Copernican model has a clear indication of which path to follow?' added the founder, pulling back the cowl from his head.

Lord Dee recruited Rufius at the age of fourteen and more years had past than either of them cared to remember. In all that time, his steely-eyed face had hardly changed, retaining a timeless quality. No one knew how old the man was, or dared to ask. It was one benefit of time travel, the ageing process was dramatically reduced.

'It's not that simple,' Eddington began, regaining his composure. 'The differential fluctuates between minor fractions of a percentage and there's also the matter of the strange attractor, which is making the equation impossible to stabilise.'

'Strange attractor?'

Eddington nodded. 'Yes, my Lord. The timeline causing the deviation appears to be chaotic. Their chronology shifts when observed, all we know that they originate from the twenty-first century.'

'Rough guess?' asked the Draconian Grandmaster Derado, with a slight smirk.

'We do not deal in guesses,' replied Eddington cooly. 'When the fate of the future hangs in the balance.'

Derado shrugged. 'You've obviously never spent any time in the dark ages.'

Eddington ignored the comment and carried on. 'The only advice I can offer you is that a watchman should be chosen to assess the situation.'

The founder looked over to Rufius. 'But, surely this falls under the jurisdiction of Westinghouse?'

The professor nodded. 'It does, my Lord, but in such as sensitive situation, I wondered if we should use someone with a more delicate touch? Especially after the Romanov incident.'

Rufius rose from his seat, his hands bunching into fists. 'How bloody dare you!'

Caitlin took his hand and squeezed it.

The founder stroked his beard into a point. 'Rufius Westinghouse has served us diligently for longer than I care to remember. He knows the twentieth centuries better than anyone. I can think of no better watchman for this task.'

'But he's a drunk!' Eddington protested. 'He should have retired decades ago.'

The founder held up his hand to silence him. 'Let us put it to the vote. All in favour of assigning this mission to Master Westinghouse, raise your hands.'

The response was unanimous. Every Grandmaster put their hand into the air.

Rufius breathed a sigh of relief and turned towards Caitlin with tears in his eyes.

'Then this session is adjourned unless the members of the council have anything further to add?'

The others shook their heads.

'Then I leave it in your good hands, Master Westinghouse,' the founder said, his blue eyes flashing. 'And trust you to consider this mission your highest priority.'

The Infinity Engines continues with Anachronist. Click here to continue the story.

Other books in the Infinity Engines universe.

The Infinity Engines

1. Anachronist
2. Maelstrom
3. Eschaton
4. Aeons
5. Tesseract
6. Contagion
7. Tempest

Infinity Engines Origins

Chimæra

Changeling

Infinity Engines Missions

1776

1888

Victoria Rex

ABOUT THE AUTHOR

For more information about The Infinity Engines series and other Here Be Dragons books please visit: www.infinityengines.com

Thank you!
Andy x

ACKNOWLEDGMENTS

Thank you to everyone who helped put this together. To Simon for giving me great feedback on this story and my wife, who continues to support me on this journey.

This is a short story in the Infinity Engines seven book series, if you enjoyed this story please check out the main series.

Made in United States
Troutdale, OR
03/16/2025

29796414R00059